To Morgan,
My new friend,
Harriet Fishel

I Wonder...

By Harriet Fishel
Illustrated by Jim Nuttle

Shooting Star Edition
American Literary Press

www.americanliterarypress.com

For Ryan, Jordyn, Samantha,
Carly and Amanda, you
make my heart beat !
Mimi

Library of Congress Cataloging in Publication Data
ISBN-13: 978-1-56167-995-9
Printed in China

I wonder… if numbers and
letters, alike, quit doing their jobs,
just all went on strike!

Or, even if colors and sounds, just
the same, got jumbled and funny,
oh my, things would change!

What would I hear,
or what would I see?
I wonder how different
my whole life would be?

Sara

If there
were no

If there were no "5",
oh my, what a giggle,
my hands couldn't wave,
and my toes wouldn't wiggle!

The sun that hugs tightly
with 5 warming rays,
might turn day into nightly,
if "5" went away.

All the beautiful clovers
with leaves up to 4,
would only have 3,
if "4" were no more.

And what would all
of the animals do,
if instead of 4 legs,
were walking on 2?

Triangles would wobble,
how wrong that would be!
They'd have only 2 sides
if there were no "3".

While the 3 little bears
that live in the forest,
would just have 2 beds,
and 2 bowls for their porridge.

Without number "2"
we would all be in trouble.
We could only have singles,
and never have doubles!

2 eyes or 2 ears
or 2 holes in my nose.
I could never give up
even any of those!

Number "1" is the most
important of all,
although, really quite little,
stands up straight and tall.

It's as big as a mountain,
and deep as the sea,
as warm as the sunshine,
as strong as a tree!

No number "1"……….
That could never be.
Cause I'm number "1,"
number "1" is Me!

So, "5" is quite special,
and "4's" just the same.
Without number "3",
would be such a shame.

No number "2", I'd be
so very glum.
But we just couldn't be
without Number "1."

If the Cows Quit their jobs

What if the cows that
make milk everyday,
decided to quit
and just play in the hay?

I know what would happen,
we'd have nothing to cheer,
cause all of our milk
would soon disappear.

I couldn't eat cookies
or cupcakes, I think.
I barely could swallow
with no milk to drink.

And what if the bees said, "We're sorry, NO MORE! We won't make the honey you buy in the store."

When sneezing, and wheezing,
and coughing, you see,
my Mommy puts honey
in my cup of tea.

It makes me feel better,
so sweet in my tummy.
I'd be so very sad
if there were no honey.

And sheep cannot ever
quit cutting their hair.
They make all the wool
for the sweaters I wear.

On cold, winter nights
my wool blankets so snug.
It helps me feel warm
like a kiss and a hug.

Without Mrs. Hen
a big mess would arise.
The eggs that she lays
are a wonderful prize!

I eat them for breakfast,
so good in my belly,
I eat them with toast
full of butter and jelly.

So, if all cows and bees
stopped doing their chores,
and the hens and the sheep
didn't work anymore,

we wouldn't have honey,
no milk or no eggs.
Without wool in the winter,
we'd have cold arms and legs.

Stop!

I know what to do
for the hens and the bees,
and all cows and sheep,

YOU MUST LISTEN...PLEASE!

First, go have a party
with ice cream and cake,
where you'll wiggle and giggle,
and shimmy and shake!

Then take a good rest, and
when you awake,
you'll share, once again,
all those things that you make!

still

I ∧ Wonder...